THE WEREWOLF SMUT:

A Thrilling Short Erotic Story

Jorge Smith

Table Of Contents

I

The warmth of spring was making Melissa sweat as she traversed the perimeter of the hunting region.

All alpha blooded wolves were allocated to a given region, and lesser ranking wolves participated in another. She smelt hundreds of various odors, all feminine yet. The girls were free to walk throughout the zone clad in a plain white shirt until The Hunting commenced.

The shirt was a technique enabling the guys to discover their partner easier; the woman would set it down on a clearing before the ritual started.

Putting it on the grass, Melissa saw the great quantity of juvenile she-wolfs this year. She noticed as they would bite their nails in a nervous habit and smell their anxiety, they were also attempting to cover their nakedness as well as they could.

'Better be terrified gals, it'll help you run faster.' She thought while standing proud waiting for the beginning signal.

From far away she could hear the roaring of the incoming guys. They were on their way to start soon after the girls departed.

A horn blasted loudly, signifying the start of The Hunting and Melissa swiftly transformed into her dark brown wolf, dashing into the forest.

Two hours into the Hunting and Melissa had successfully avoided meeting any interested guys. There were a lot of younger male wolves, so she as a veteran could zigzag her way through the woods, without being disturbed, since they would chase down the young and inexperienced females.

The domain was wide but not limitless so she had to be cautious to shift away from pathways where she might detect strong male odors.

Melissat took a breath and stopped for a few minutes. It would be too exhausting to run for the full period of the 24 hours the Hunting lasted, but she attempted to never linger at one location too long, since her powerful smell would attach to her surroundings readily.

A rustling sound nearby had her spring into action once more. A definite male fragrance followed immediately and she picked up some snarling with her keen ears. Getting scared she fled at fast speed towards the opposite way.

The female noticed a strong aura to her right, as a male wolf pursued her. She thought it unusual that he kept himself slightly to the side instead of sprinting straight behind her.

She could not tell how long she was traveling at that rate but at some time she lost track of her follower's smell. It must suggest that he either followed another road, or lost interest.

Getting a bit slower, Melissat listened intently. There was a rushing sound of water coming from her right. A creek was running there, quietly abandoned.

She opted to go by the creek, since the odds of an unanticipated assault were lesser.

The aroma of someone was lingering, but she could not determine whether it was recent. As the fragrance did not fade after a time the she-wolf grew a bit more mindful of it. It felt curiously gratifying, but too faint to say more.

It was slowly starting to become dark, suggesting that around five hours must have gone since the beginning, yet the aroma was still surrounding her, tormenting her nose by only barely stimulating her senses.

Melissat decided to adjust her course, since the sound of the river was toning out the sound of any predators, which was risky now that nightfall was diminishing her sight.

She heard growls from far away along with moans of mating wolves. The farther she was walking, the more she felt anxiety crawling up her spine.

Never before at the Hunting had she felt like that, her wolf started to feel on edge, losing awareness of the direction she was racing.

Her heart was racing quickly as she went close to a fence made of silver that was erected around the region, and it started to beat even faster when she saw that it was joining with another fence from the west, making a corner.

She groaned internally at her stupidity to practically allow herself to be trapped. The fragrance of her relentless following became a bit stronger and with with it came another understanding;

The aroma belonged to an extraordinarily strong man, who appeared to be highly compatible with her.

II

Melissa's insides were uneasy and she had to struggle with her inner wolf who wanted to remain still and wait for her future mate. During the process she stumbled over some roots and nearly smashed against the silver fence, scorching a few of the top strands of her fur. But the odor of that didn't distract her enough to ignore the fact that she could not run, she had no option but to confront her attacker.

For the first time in her life she felt dubious about her talents. The possible tie between her and the unknown guy was already interfering with her head and senses so it would be one hell of a struggle with her wolf to first fight him, then outrun him.

The female peered around, it was unusually silent. Only the moon was shining above her through the tree's branches, affording little to no sight of her companion but she could feel his eyes looking at her; He could see her, but she could not see him.

Getting into a defensive stance she bared her fangs and ruffled her fur up to make her seem even larger. Her shape was rather huge compared to other females and the alpha blood scorching through her veins could make any lesser ranking wolf shudder in dread.

To her sorrow the male wolf did not budge an inch, she could still feel the searing look he had on her.

His perfume had an intoxicating effect on her, filling up her nose and clouding her thinking.

Melissa could not believe how profoundly she was impacted by this man. She had met a few wolves that were mildly compatible with her, but never did she feel like she was losing control of her wolf and senses.

As anxiety ate her up from within, the concealed wolf moved closer, making a few dry leafs crunch beneath his massive paws.

Now the female could see golden eyes sparkling and enormous black ears twitching. His shape was hunkered down between shrubs, however there was no mistake that he was exceptionally huge.

His sheer alpha force was smashing in waves towards the she-wolf, seeking to make her surrender. Any other girl would have but Melissa had strong blood in her veins as well, helping her hold solid in her position.

She let out a loud guttural growl at the man, only to receive an even lower growl in reply. The jet black fur of the wolf was reflecting the moon's light, making it look inky and giving him a strange air as he took two long steps towards her direction.

Melissa terrified, he didn't appear fazed at all by her protective response, she did not know what to do in order to keep his big black bulk away from her.

She attempted snapping towards his direction, getting ready to attack on him, but her wolf and the sight of his monstrously big teeth were keeping her back.

Sensing her uncertainty, the man continued to circle her carefully, still slightly squatting and taking in every inch of her being with his analytical eyes. He also took the opportunity to sniff at her tail which prompted the female to swiftly pull it between her legs after snapping her teeth at him. One of her teeth touched his snout, producing a small line of blood.

The black alpha roared earth shaking as he leapt at her with the the speed of light, pulling the she-wolf down with his claws and teeth forcibly burrowing into the hair and tiny fat on her neck, forcefully making her surrender. He didn't anticipate Melissa to snarl and flail about, so he instantly reinforced his grasp on her neck, causing a little blood to trickle into the forest ground.

'Shift.'

His rich heavy voice battled its way into her thoughts via a freshly created connection, made possible by the bond sparking at their contact.

Electric sparks were building between their bodies, although the terrible grasp of his fangs and paws on her neck and abdomen were somewhat masking the emotions.

The dark brown she-wolf was playing with her life at this point; She could continue to thrash and turn until he eventually bit through important parts of her neck making her slowly but surely bleed out, or submit to him by shifting into her human form.

'Shift!'

Demanded his suddenly very much agitated sounding voice. The male was tremendously shocked at the resistance and determination this female exhibited, but her reluctance was putting his wolf on edge and making his tolerance run thin after all the hours he had been tracking her.

Finally the sound of bones snapping could be heard as the mystery guy released her neck and took a step back.

In front of him now sat the nude body of Melissa Blake, her dark brown hair tangled and a frantic look on her face.

He gazed into her piercing green eyes, then her sinfully beautiful physique and could not find a single area on her that wasn't completely exquisite and attractive to him.

Slowly he moved closer, head dropping low to carefully sniff her body with his large nose. Beginning at her feet Melissa could feel his cool nose brushing against her flesh, causing sparks to flare at the spot.

She pushed her feet away from his nose while gazing at him harder.

She did not enjoy the idea that she had to submit to him, after all she never had to do it in her entire life. She felt vulnerable, bewildered and furious at the things this guy was making her feel; attracted, inebriated, dominated,... aroused.

As his nose was working its way up her legs, she felt her lower tummy burn as she was slowly and unconsciously growing aroused. The black wolf let out a low growl at the fragrance reaching his nose and moved back a bit.

After a pause and a few gasping breaths he started his investigation at her stomach. The sensations of his touch, even just the slightest were torturing Melissa as she didn't know if she wanted to run for the hills or wanted him to mate her already. The thoughts of her and her wolf were clashing while she was enjoying, then hating the touch of her predator.

Said predator was starting to sniff and caress her breasts at which the female wrapped her hand over his nose, preventing him from moving.

She gazed into his flaming eyes while hissing at him, daring him once more.

Feral instincts were ruling the black wolf who was profoundly allured and likewise aroused by the female. He could not understand why she was still battling him.

Growling with his closed snout he forced his way to her neck, effortlessly pushing despite the constraint of her hand and showing her that she was utterly defenseless at the time.

When his canine grazed her delicate human flesh, Melissa unhappily succumbed to him again by releasing his snout and averted her sight.

There was a change in the air as she briefly gave up the struggle with her own wolf, her green eyes going a few shades darker, signaling that for now her animalistic side was in charge.

After some time the glare evolved into gazing and her fingers delicately caressed the fur on his head.

Ironically the large alpha wolf let out a purr of joy. Finally the she-wolf appeared to surrender into the mating attraction so finally he too could change into his human form.

Soon the wolf legs that were caging Melissa transformed into muscular arms on each side of her head and a strong toned human torso was hovering over her's.

She peered up at his face, quite thrilled with magnificent, manly features and dark gray eyes hidden by strands of black hair, looking back at her.

The handsome man could smell her arousal growing at the sight of his looks and smirked cockily. His arousal on the other hand, was obvious the instant he drew in her aroma a while ago, now faintly pushing at her lower tummy each time Melissa took a breath.

"Oliver Gray."

He gave her his name in a hoarse voice, waiting anxiously for her's as well.

"Melissa Blake."

She responded with her husky voice quivering accidentally.

Slowly but resolute Oliver went down to kiss her, at which the female still hesitated. Her human side returned when they switched their identities and she still wasn't too keen on mating even though the Grays were now a highly powerful lineage with a strong pack.

His reputation as Alpha was fairly good also and no one dared to offend him. The only thing that was holding Melissa back was her pride. She never liked being controlled or dominated but Alpha Oliver Gray was doing just that and the fact that she was aroused by it annoyed the female to no end..

III

Melissa shifted her head to the side, avoiding his lips.

Oliver felt her hesitancy which infuriated him and drove up his dominant wolf. She plainly found him appealing however she didn't want to give in freely.

He held her chin pulling her face to his while pushing part of the weight of his abdomen onto her, producing a sizzling feeling between their bodies.

"Stop fighting, Melissa."

It was a warning whispered in a low voice before he forced his lips over hers.

When she didn't respond, he grabbed her chin further, snarling quietly. The vibrations of the growl excited her breasts that were mashed against his chest, which forced her to involuntarily let out a groan.

Oliver grinned against her lips, seizing her opening mouth as an opportunity to deepen the kiss.

Slowly he released her chin when he realized that she again lost control to her wolf and slipped his fingers down her body all the way to her femininity.

Rubbing it with two long fingers, he felt the moisture between her folds and snarled deeply, making her groan again. The man continued rubbing his fingers over her clit, carefully building to an orgasm as her moaning became louder.

...

"Do you want me?"

Oliver inquired slyly, knowing she wasn't in control and near the point of an orgasm.

"Ahh..."

Melissa wasn't in her proper frame of mind, the feelings of the link were making her feel like she was in paradise with angels singing.

"Tell me, baby."

He encouraged her to say it, while tormenting her with extremely slow strokes on her clit.

"I wa- ahh..."

She could hardly form a phrase so Oliver halted his motions. Instantly her dark clouded eyes were on his, silently questioning why he stopped.

"Tell me that you desire me."

Oliver repeated forcefully after sneering at her.

The silence and his face roused Melissa from her high, regaining control of her thoughts and body. A frown was finding its way on her face.

She felt upset at herself for allowing herself to be misled and taunted by him.

"Fuck you."

She said, venom infusing her words.

Taken back by her change of conduct he withdrew his hand from her femininity and wrapped it around her neck.

His wolf was upset and unhappy that the she-wolf wouldn't allow him mate her and repeatedly fought back, even after he proved his might and dominance to her.

His eyes were practically dark as he stole a bit of her breath away by gripping her neck with his enormous palm.

Melissa snarled at him, but her desire was still palpable in the air.

"You won't back down, huh?"

Oliver arched an eyebrow at her, knowing that if he wouldn't be forceful with her, the tough female would stay hesitant to mate.

It definitely excited her while he was manhandling her so he resolved to let his wolf take control entirely.

Melissa couldn't respond even if she wanted to, his palm was pushing her neck too tight.

The instant she saw that his wolf had seized control she was scared because she knew there was no question they would be married in a matter of minutes now.

She felt the tip of his huge dick nudge against her core as she peered quite hopelessly into his dark lust filled eyes.

Oliver leaned over her body situating himself at her entrance and his lips at her neck, ready to brand her at any moment.

He ultimately let Melissa breathe and stabilized himself with his hands on the ground, before ramming his dick between her folds in one rapid move, giving her no time to get acclimated to his girth as his wolf was anxious and frantic now.

The female screamed out of pain and since she was still furious she grasped his shoulders with extended claws, scraping his flesh and causing blood to flow.

As a result Oliver hissed and softly bit her neck while driving into her at a vicious and increasingly furious tempo.

His grunts and her moans of evident pleasure were filling the peacefulness of the night.

It was immoral, but blissfully pleasant for Melissa. She was being pushed down on the ground and forcibly thrusted into, but she felt nothing but excited by it.

It was her fault too, triggering the Alpha over and over again, till he lost control to his wolf, who of course wouldn't be as nice as his human counterpart, not gentle at all.

Olivers sharp fangs scraped the delicate flesh on her neck more than once, showing his intention to brand her as his. He gasped deeply when he felt the female's core constrict around his cock as she was ready to come undone underneath him.

Melissa screamed and cried, her thighs trembling fiercely, claws sinking into the hard muscles of Olivers back, before orgasming all over him.

The grunts of ecstasy coming from the man were earthshaking and he felt himself being near to his release as well.

The she-wolf slowly came down from her high, merely to feel an increasing pressure within her walls, straining them farther, to a painful degree.

"Ah, stop.."

She moaned, her oversensitive femininity feeling as though being torn apart.

Oliver on the other hand was utterly out of control of his activities, pursuing his climax as the knot at the base of his twitching dick swelled and grew further, ultimately reaching too huge so that it caught within the female's cunt.

"Stop, please..."

Her screams filled the air, matching his shouts of delight.

That's when the hot liquid of his semen began gushing deep into her, filling her up, while the male snarled and whimpered into her neck, the most powerful climax of his life sweeping over him just after he dug his teeth deep into the side of her neck.

Melissa couldn't hold back the scream that followed his movements, intense agony sweeping over her body, as Oliver was being anything but delicate with his massive fangs.

After the first agony of the bite, a low soothing burn was beginning to replace it, creeping through her body like a narcotic until she was feeling elated by the tie blossoming between the two wolves, joining them together forever.

The she-wolf could feel his emotions, his anger and desire for her, but most of all his deep appreciation for her strength and confidence..

IV

Slowly both freshly wedded wolves cooled down after their finished union and Oliver's massive body started to feel quite heavy against Melissa's.

She nudged his body a bit, attempting to rouse her lover from his sleep.

He received the message and turned over next to her, but since they were still attached owing to his knot deep within her femininity, she awkwardly was pulled along, falling partially on top of him.

"Ow, hey!"

She moaned, as her painful walls were stretched again.

"Sorry!"

Oliver shouted, fairly delighted, staring at his beauty on top of him.

Melissa averted his gaze, feeling startled and still furious despite the freshy created link sending soothing hormones and love pheromones out to their bodies.

When she couldn't stand his look anymore, she slammed her palms down onto his chest, matching his eyes.

"How long do we have to remain like this?!"

" 'until I'll be ready for round two."

...

The bewildered look she flashed at him, was precisely what he anticipated, but her speechlessness made him giggle.

She fought to find words, as her human half was itching to put him in his place, while her wolf side was struggling and purring in desire at his words.

"N-No way are you going to fuck me again on this dirty ground without my will!"

Oliver laughed at her tone, before sneakily grinning and stroking a hand down her spine, making her shudder.

"Oh, I don't think it will be against your will."

"Why would you think that?!"

She did her best to seem furious, but his fingers stroking her ass were placing filthy images in her head.

Oliver murmured, the vibrations exciting her nipples that were squeezed against his chest.

"Maybe because I can feel what you're thinking right now?"

The female's cheeks became a rose tone due to her hurried condition, a combination of a moan and a growl exiting her lips out of displeasure. Her companion was still grinning, loving every minute of it.

Oliver moved a bit in his location under his companion, sensing that the knot had almost fully dissolved.

The action made Melissa scream instinctively and she bit her lip to stop herself from letting out further humiliating noises, until he gently withdrew himself out of her soaking core by pulling her up a little.

The instant she glanced down and realized that his cock was as erect as before they married, she visibly gasped.

"I wasn't joking about being ready for round two."

His deep voice stunned her as their gazes connected and despite his remarks, he looked pretty warmly at her.

The night was dark and peaceful, the moon reflecting in his gray eyes, turning them silver.

Never before had Melissa felt so vulnerable and flustered but at the same time safe with a male.

Their lips connected, but this time it wasn't as aggressive and hungry as the last time they did.

It was soft and tender, new, more loving emotions of need and want being exchanged between the mates.

It continued until the obstinate female pushed away with a huff and separated their bodies by standing up. She wobbled a bit on her feet, but caught herself in time.

Oliver remained resting on the ground, his erection standing proudly, as he watched his partner wincing when both her and his come slowly flowed down her legs.

His eyes became a familiar color of dark gray, when she attempted to wipe it away with her hands, only causing the white sticky substance to ooze all over her legs and hands.

Melissas didn't even see him getting up and yelled as he slammed her back into a nearby tree.

"What do you think you're doing?"

His voice was husky and trembling from the guttural growl that was forcing its way out of his throat at the same time.

"I-I... I feel sticky."

Her stuttering voice sounded foreign even to her own ears, as she tried to calm her mate by stroking his chest carefully.

Another growl filled the air before the male leaned his head into her neck and started to lick his mark on her.

The dried blood tasted metallic on his tongue and Melissa began to shudder violently owing to the sensitivity of the region.

"You're mine."

He remarked with an animalistic tone after washing the spot carefully. When the female didn't respond he pushed her deeper into the tree and peered into her eyes, as she gasped.

"You're only mine,"

Oliver virtually snarled the words at her, till she was a quivering wreck.

"Say it!"

"I-I'm yours!"

She blurted out, a bit startled by his scream of possessiveness.

"I'm only yours, Oliver."

She whispered as he visibly relaxed at her words, breaking eye contact only to continue to lick her mark.

Melissa couldn't hold back the moan from the sensations erupting at her neck.

She felt the man squeezing his body even closer to hers, his cock poking against her stomach. He worked his way up to her jaw, to her lips, hungrily kissing her against the tree. His hands were following her body from her breast gently down to her ass.

The scent of new arousal was clouding his head once more, forcing his wolf to emerge.

"Oliver..."

She wasn't necessarily attempting to fight him off, but his wolf responded quickly, spinning her around so that her front was forced against the tree and his cock slammed into her ass.

Growls were coming from him like a wild wolf out of control and Melissa was breathing hard, starting to fear the agony that was going to come.

She felt his canines on the unharmed side of her neck, as he positioned his dick at her entrance.

The she-wolf's hand reached out behind her to lightly push against his hip, hoping he understood the message to go easier on her sore womanhood.

He snarled quietly, but appeared to sustain a slower pace this time. She felt his tip make its way between her folds as she retained the grip on his hip to slow him down as much as she could.

It was much more delicate than last time but he bit into the unmarked side of her neck rather forcefully to vent out his displeasure elsewhere.

When he filled her up completely, his length stretching her walls as she got used to his size, he couldn't hold back any longer.

He quickly pulled out of her pussy, just to ram his way back inside so that his balls slapped against her clit.

Melissa moaned so loud, she thought it could be heard from miles away.

Oliver set a harsh and quick pace, hitting her g-spot each time he thrusted into her.

He growled when she came all over him the second time that day, her legs trembling and almost giving out if not for his steely grip on her hips.

He rode out her climax by continuing to pound at her place, till she collapsed limb against the tree, sobbing from oversensitivity but Oliver wasn't done yet.

He gripped her neck from behind and dragged her body closer to his, making her back arch and his dick drive even further within.

The female howled out of agony and ecstasy, grasping the tree with extended claws, leaving deep scratches behind.

"Ahh, Oliver s-stop,"

She blurted out breathlessly, as his grasp on her neck seemed to tighten, each time he smashed into her.

"Ugh, can't breathe.."

Her murmurs were overwhelmed by the groans that were coming out of the male's lips, yet his grasp on her neck was sliding slightly owing to the perspiration developing, enabling her to get some breath.

Melissa could feel another orgasm building up and impulsively bit her lip with extended canines so that blood was flowing down her chin into Olivers fingers.

He responded by moving her head a bit to kiss her hungrily, tasting her blood on his tongue.

His other hand pushed into her waist to hold her motionless as he slammed into her cunt so hard that her entire body started to quake.

By now, the bark of the tree had ripped off, resting on the ground as the she-wolf had clawed on it so frantically while seeking her climax.

It came crashing down on both of them, Olivers cock knotting so quickly this time, he didn't even realize he was this close to come.

He felt both his and her orgasm intertwine via their relationship, generating explosive ecstatic emotions in rhythm and tripling the pleasure for both of them.

He had to hold the tree too in order to keep grounded, panting into the girl's neck and drinking in her enticing aroma.

"Shit,.."

He mumbled when he realized that Melissa was practically unconscious in his hold.

The chase, so much stress, three intense orgasms and a mark were probably a bit much for her to handle in that short span of time.

The male wolf wrapped his arms around her form, turning them around and carefully sliding down the tree to sit against it, because they were still connected by his knot like the last time.

Oliver gazed down at his mate, feeling a little guilty all of a sudden, now that his human side was back in control.

V

Melissa made it apparent to the unknown Wolf that she didn't want to be mated straight from the start.

She resisted him even while she was being betrayed by her own body.

He sort of forcefully mated her, not once but twice and marked her throughout the process.

Her pleadings for him to stop were ignored at that time, but today he recalls them perfectly.

He simply couldn't control himself and his wolf.

Never previously had he exhibited particular attention in any she-wolf until he sniffed her clothes on the clearing, driven by her scent for hours.

Then, when she exhibited so much resistance, his wolf felt challenged in his strength and dominance, needing to make her submit, having to make her his; with or without her human side's approval.

On the other hand they were supposed to be. The relationship between them is strong from the start, influencing them greatly. Two great lineages coming together, it couldn't be more suitable.

And Oliver simply couldn't let her go after putting his eyes on her, a more patient and loving mating procedure was rendered difficult by the ladies resistance and his domineering possessiveness.

Carefully he attempted to slide out of his mate, the knot had dissolved, making it easier but the action caused Melissa to come back to awareness. She tilted her head to gaze up at him, feeling his sympathy and a trace of humiliation via their linked tie.

"I can take no more..."

She whispered, her voice raspy from all the shouting and wailing.

Oliver stared at her pitifully and brushed her face lighty with his palm.

His once proud and confident companion was suddenly so weak and subservient, it nearly wounded him.

"I'm sorry."

He peered at her, probing her emotions for any traces of the typical rage, but there was simply submissiveness crashing in waves towards him.

"I'll try not to do anything without your agreement anymore."

His remarks caused Melissa's heart to flutter, a more loving expression across her face.

"I'm sorry I couldn't control myself, I harmed you." He continued.

The she-wolf reached out to grasp her mates chin, bringing him down to plant a delicate kiss on his lips.

"I may not have wanted it and you injured me, but I'm yours now. There's no going back."

Oliver's heart softened at her words, a grin finding its way onto his face, before he buried his face into the hair cascading over her neck.

"I'll defend and adore you for the rest of my life, Melissa Blake."

He muttered the vow into her hair.

The End